This edition first published in 1999 by
Floris Books, 15 Harrison Gardens, Edinburgh.
Story © Evelien van Dort / Christofoor, Zeist 1999
Illustrations © Veronica Nahmias / Christofoor, Zeist 1999
British Library CIP Data available.   ISBN 0-86315-301-1
Printed in Belgium

The Chicken who Wanted to Fly

A story by Evelien van Dort
Illustrated by Veronica Nahmias

Floris Books

There was once a little brown hen. Together with the other hens and the brightly-coloured cock she lived in a hen-house on the farm.

Every night the hens slept safely in the hen-house, sitting in a row.

During the day the hens ran about freely all over the farmer's garden, around the meadow and along the edges of the hazel-wood.

The little brown hen liked to wander by
herself into the wood and watch the birds flying
among the trees. How she would love to stay there
and live like the birds, as free as the air! She wanted to fly,
just like them, and perch high up in the trees.

When the sun went down that evening,
the cock stood as usual watching the hens go into the hen-house
for the night. The little brown hen was always the last.

Tucked up in the hen-house, the little brown hen put her head into her feathers. All night she dreamed she was sitting on a high branch among the green leaves of the hazel-wood.

"Cock-a-doodle-doo!" cried the cock, "Wake up!"
It was time to get up. Outside it was already quite light.

One by one the hens stirred and shook
themselves. They came tripping out of the hen-house
and went scratching and pecking through the garden.

That day the little brown hen rushed off
as usual to the hazel-wood. She looked for a low
branch and tried as hard as she could to fly up to it.
She fluttered and fell a few times, then at last
she reached the branch and balanced there. What fun!

At the end of the day the cock called the hens back
for the night. But the little brown hen didn't want to go back
in the hen-house. She hid in the hazel-wood.

In the twilight, the little brown hen flew up to her branch. She was so pleased and excited! Two little birds above twittered: "You're not very safe down there. Are you sure that's a good idea?"

The little brown hen looked up and clucked at them. "Mind your own business and go to sleep."

It was growing dark.
As happy as anything, the little brown hen
settled down on her branch. No cock, no one to bother her.
How peaceful it was there in the wood! She nestled her head
into her warm feathers and dozed off.

Crackle, crackle, whisper, whisper ...

The little brown hen woke with a start. It was completely dark. Where was that noise coming from? Anxiously she peered down. Below her something was moving.

Then she remembered the rats with their long sharp teeth. They often came to nibble the hen food and the cock always chased them away.

Quick! Back to the hen-house!
Fluttering to the ground, she shot off as fast
as she could and dashed up the plank and through the little door to safety.

She squeezed in between the other hens. They were all fast asleep.

It had been quite an adventure in the hazel-wood, she thought, but now it was good to be safe and warm at home again.